PUFFIN BOOKS

The Mouse Family
Robinson

Dick King-Smith served in the Grenadier Guards during the Second World War, and afterwards spent twenty years as a farmer in Gloucestershire, the county of his birth. Many of his stories are inspired by his farming experiences. Later he taught at a village primary school. His first book, *The Fox Busters*, was published in 1978. Since then he has written a great number of children's books, including *The Sheep-Pig* (winner of the Guardian Award and filmed as *Babe*), *Harry's Mad*, *Noah's Brother*, *The Hodgeheg*, *Martin's Mice*, *Ace*, *The Cuckoo Child* and *Harriet's Hare* (winner of the Children's Book Award in 1995). At the British Book Awards in 1991 he was voted Children's Author of the Year. He has three children, a large number of grandchildren and several great-grandchildren, and lives in a seventeenth-century cottage only a crow's-flight fro͞   ͞rn.

D0279690

Books by Dick King-Smith

ACE
BLESSU
DINOSAUR SCHOOL
DINOSAUR TROUBLE
DUMPLING
FAT LAWRENCE
FIND THE WHITE HORSE
THE FOX BUSTERS
GEORGE SPEAKS
THE GOLDEN GOOSE
HARRY'S MAD
THE HODGEHEG
THE INVISIBLE DOG
THE JENIUS
MAGNUS POWERMOUSE
MARTIN'S MICE
THE MOUSE FAMILY ROBINSON
POPPET
THE QUEEN'S NOSE
THE SCHOOLMOUSE
THE SHEEP-PIG
SMASHER
THE SWOOSE
UNDER THE MISHMASH TREES
THE WATER HORSE

GLOUCESTERSHIRE COUNTY LIBRARY	
993159886 7	
PETERS	07-Mar-08
	£4.99

The Mouse Family
Robinson

Dick King-Smith

Illustrated by Ben Cort

PUFFIN

PUFFIN BOOKS

Published by the Penguin Group
Penguin Books Ltd, 80 Strand, London WC2R ORL, England
Penguin Group (USA) Inc., 375 Hudson Street, New York, New York 10014, USA
Penguin Group (Canada), 90 Eglinton Avenue East, Suite 700, Toronto, Ontario, Canada M4P 2Y3
(a division of Pearson Penguin Canada Inc.)
Penguin Ireland, 25 St Stephen's Green, Dublin 2, Ireland (a division of Penguin Books Ltd)
Penguin Group (Australia), 250 Camberwell Road, Camberwell, Victoria 3124, Australia
(a division of Pearson Australia Group Pty Ltd)
Penguin Books India Pvt Ltd, 11 Community Centre, Panchsheel Park, New Delhi – 110 017, India
Penguin Group (NZ), 67 Apollo Drive, Rosedale, North Shore 0632, New Zealand
(a division of Pearson New Zealand Ltd)
Penguin Books (South Africa) (Pty) Ltd, 24 Sturdee Avenue, Rosebank, Johannesburg 2196, South Africa

Penguin Books Ltd, Registered Offices: 80 Strand, London WC2R ORL, England

puffinbooks.com

First published 2007
Published in this edition 2008

1

Text copyright © Fox Busters Ltd, 2007
Illustrations copyright © Ben Cort, 2007
All rights reserved

The moral right of the author and illustrator has been asserted

Set in Perpetua
Typeset by Palimpsest Book Production Limited,
Grangemouth, Stirlingshire
Made and printed in England by Clays Ltd, St Ives plc

Except in the United States of America, this book is sold subject to the condition
that it shall not, by way of trade or otherwise, be lent, re-sold, hired out, or otherwise
circulated without the publisher's prior consent in any form of binding or cover other than
that in which it is published and without a similar condition including this condition being
imposed on the subsequent purchaser

British Library Cataloguing in Publication Data
A CIP catalogue record for this book is available from the British Library

ISBN: 978-0-141-32062-5

Chapter One

John Robinson and Mr Brown were next-door neighbours. That is to say, they both lived under the kitchen floor, for John Robinson and Mr Brown were housemice.

John was a young chap. He was respectful towards his neighbour, who was very old, and always addressed him as 'Mr Brown'. Mr Brown, John knew, now lived alone because his wife had been eaten by the cat.

There came an evening when John's young wife, Janet, told him that he was to become a father for the first time. She was tearing up bits of newspaper to make a comfy nest.

'Gosh!' said John. 'You mean you're going to have a baby?'

'Babies,' said Janet.

She has got fat lately, come to think of it, said John to himself.

'When?' he asked.

'Very soon.'

'Gosh! How many?'

'How do I know, you stupid mouse,' said Janet. 'Now push off, do, and leave me in peace.'

As John was hurrying under the kitchen floor, he met his neighbour coming back home.

'Good evening, Mr Brown,' he said.

'Evening, John,' said Mr Brown. 'How's life?'

'Wonderful!' replied John. 'I am going to be a father.'

'For the first time, eh?'

'Yes, I believe you've had a large number of children, Mr Brown, haven't you?'

'Dozens. So many that I've gone and forgotten most of their names. My late wife and I used to rely on the alphabet.'

'The alphabet?' said John.

'Yes. Start with A – Adam, let's say, or Alice – and keep going till you get to Z. That gives you twenty-six names.'

'You mean you've had twenty-six
children, Mr Brown?'

'Seventy-eight, actually, John. We
went through the alphabet three
times.'

'Gosh!' said John.

'Xs and Zs,' said Mr Brown, 'are the
hardest ones to put names to, but we

managed. Why don't you try the same trick?'

'I will, I will,' said John. 'Thanks, Mr Brown, that's a good idea.'

The young mouse and his elderly neighbour chatted for a while, mainly about food. A nest under the kitchen floor, as both knew well, is the best place for mice to live. Those clumsy giants called humans were always dropping bits of food on the floor, and if a mouse was bold enough, there were lovely things to eat in the larder.

Talking about food made John feel hungry and after a while he said, 'I must be going, Mr Brown, if you'll excuse me.'

'Of course, John,' Mr Brown replied, 'and I'm so pleased to hear your good news. Please give my regards to your wife.'

'I will,' replied John, 'and thank you.'

Poor old fellow, he thought, remembering what had happened to Mrs Brown.

Now evening had turned to night, and the giants had all gone up the stairs to bed. John Robinson popped out of a mousehole and began to search the kitchen floor, all his senses alert, especially for the squeak of the cat flap.

He was in luck. Someone had spilled half a dozen cornflakes: not much for a giant, but a feast for a mouse.

His hunger satisfied, he made his way home.

Will Janet have had the babies yet? he wondered. How many will there be? How many will be boys, how many girls?

The answers to these questions, John found, were 'Yes', 'Six' and 'Three of each'.

'What shall we call them?' John asked.

'You can choose, if you like,' said Janet.

I'll use Mr Brown's alphabet method, thought John. Six kids, that's A to F. Let's see now, I must think up some unusual names because I'm sure my

children will grow up to be unusual mice.

John Robinson spent the rest of the night deciding what to call his newborn sons and daughters. As dawn broke, he knew he had found six perfect names. 'And,' he said to himself, 'I must tell Mr Brown. I'm sure he'd like to know,' and he hurried along one of the runways beneath the kitchen floor.

'Mr Brown,' he said, when he had found his neighbour, 'Janet's had six babies. I thought you'd like to know.'

'Congratulations, John!' said Mr Brown. 'Got names for them?'

'I have,' said John. 'Ambrose, Beaumont, Camilla, Desdemona, Eustace and Felicity. What d'you think?'

'Brilliant!' said Mr Brown.

'Three boys and three girls, eh? It's a start. Twenty more babies and you'll have finished your first alphabet of names.'

'Gosh!' said John to himself. To think that his neighbour had seventy-eight kids!

Even as he thought this, they heard, through the floorboards above their heads, the squeak of the cat flap.

Chapter Two

At the sound the two mice froze, even though they were quite safe under the kitchen floorboards. They looked at one another and Mr Brown sighed deeply.

I know what he's thinking, said John to himself. How dreadful if such a thing ever happened to my Janet. If only that horrible cat didn't live here.

'I must be getting back to my family, Mr Brown,' he said after a while.

'Of course,' replied Mr Brown. 'I'd love to come and see them when they're a little older. Could I?'

'Please do,' said John.

The mousekins had been born naked and blind but later on, when they had grown coats of fur (grey, of course) and had opened their beady little eyes, John invited Mr Brown round. Proudly he and Janet stood on either side of their six children while the old mouse looked them over.

'They're lovely!' he said. 'I do congratulate you both.'

'Thank you,' replied Janet, and 'Thank you, sir,' said John.

'When they're a bit older,' said Mr Brown, 'perhaps they'll come and visit me?' and, a few weeks later, one of them did.

Beaumont was the brightest and the most adventurous of the six mousekins, and he was the first to venture out of the nest and start to explore the spaces under the kitchen floor. Soon he came upon a mouse run that led upwards and, following it, stuck his head out of a hole in the

skirting board. He found himself
staring across the kitchen floor. Beside
the cooker, he could see, was a
basket.

Beaumont was not only bright and
adventurous, but also curious. I
wonder what's in that basket? he
thought.

He was halfway across the kitchen
floor when two things happened.
First, he heard a voice coming from
the hole he'd just left, a frantic voice
that cried, 'Come back! Come back!
Quickly! Quickly!'

Then he saw a face, a face that rose
above the rim of the basket, a fearful

furry face with yellow eyes that were fixed upon him.

Beaumont turned and dashed back towards the hole in the skirting board just in time. Above him, he heard the scrabble of the cat's claws as it scratched at the mousehole. Before him, he saw an old mouse.

'Oh!' squeaked Beaumont. 'Was it you who called me back?'

'It was,' replied Mr Brown. 'That was a narrow squeak, young fellow. What's your name?'

'I'm Beaumont Robinson.'

'One of John's children?'

'Yes. Who are you?'

'I'm Mr Brown.'

'Oh, you're Dad's friend.'

'I like to think so.'

'The one that came to visit us?'

'Yes.'

'Have you got any children?'

'Seventy-eight,' replied Mr Brown. Though goodness only knows how many are still alive, he thought.

'Gosh!' said Beaumont (a word he had learned from his father). 'My dad told us your wife got eaten by the cat.'

'She did, Beaumont,' said Mr Brown. And so would you have been, he thought, if I hadn't happened to look out just in time. Yours would have been a very short life.

'Well,' said Beaumont, 'isn't there

any way we can get rid of the beastly
thing?'

'Alas, no,' said Mr Brown. 'Cats can

kill mice but unfortunately, mice can't kill cats.'

'Oh,' said Beaumont. 'So we've got to wait till it dies of old age, have we?'

'That might be a long time,' said Mr Brown.

'What can we do, then?'

'Nothing, I'm afraid, Beaumont. The giants have got a cat and we have got to live with it.'

Have we? thought Beaumont. What if . . . ? No, I'd better ask Dad first.

'Got to go,' he said. 'Nice talking to you, Uncle Brown.'

When he got home, he said, 'I've been talking to Uncle Brown, Dad.'

'Have you indeed?' said John. I bet the old chap's pleased at being called that, he thought.

'Yes,' said Beaumont. 'He saved my life, Dad. I went up into the kitchen and the cat nearly got me!'

'Gosh!' said John.

'Uncle Brown says we've just got to live with the beastly thing.'

'Well, he's right, Beaumont. We've got no choice.'

'Yes we have, Dad,' said Beaumont. 'If the cat won't leave us, we can leave the cat.'

'What d'you mean?'

'We can move to another house, one without a cat. We can emigrate, Dad,' said Beaumont.

Chapter Three

'Emigrate?' said John to Beaumont.

'Yes, Dad.'

'But . . . how shall I know if another house has a cat or not?'

'If it has, it'll smell of the beastly thing. If it hasn't, it won't. Simple, Dad.'

'It'll take me an awfully long time to inspect every house in the street.'

'It would if it was just you, Dad,' said Beaumont, 'but what if we all helped, eh, Mum?'

'I certainly will,' said Janet, 'but you kids are too small to take the risk.'

'We're not,' said Beaumont, turning to the other five mousekins, 'are we?

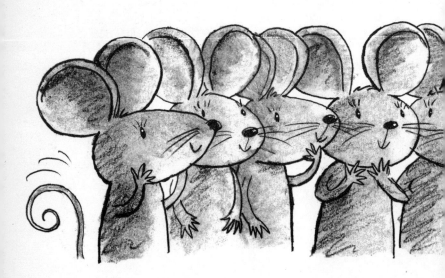

We can help, can't we?' and with one
voice Ambrose and Camilla and
Desdemona and Eustace and Felicity
cried, 'Yes!'

Janet looked proudly at her six
children.

'All right,' she said, 'but not just
yet. Wait till you've grown a lot
bigger.'

'And a lot faster on your feet,'
added John. 'There'll be other cats in
other houses in the street, and dogs
too, and then there's all the traffic.
Wait till you're as big as Mum and
me.'

'But that'll be ages, Dad!' said
Beaumont.

'Do as your father says,' said Janet
sharply, and in unison Ambrose and
Beaumont and Camilla and
Desdemona and Eustace and Felicity
muttered, 'Yes, Mum.'

In fact a month went by before John
and Janet allowed the six mousekins
out of the house.

John had established a route — from under the kitchen floor through a runway that led down into the cellar, and from the cellar up and out through a grating on to the pavement outside.

Janet made a plan of action. Their house was Number 24, even-numbered like all those on that side of the street. Each night she and the three girls would work their way down the road, somehow making their way into Number 22, then Number 20 and so on, while John and the three boys would be inspecting each house up the street – Numbers 26, 28, 30 and so on.

'Let's just hope they don't all have cats in them, Janet,' said John. 'I don't fancy having to cross the road.'

But luck was on their side.

On the fourth night Janet and the girls explored Number 16 and came

home excited and delighted to report
that there was no smell or sign of cat
or dog in that house.

'All we could smell,' said Janet, 'was mice!'

'Great!' said John. 'We'll emigrate there.'

Five of the mousekins squeaked with joy but Beaumont said, 'What about Uncle Brown?'

'What about him?' said the others.

'He'll be lonely without us.'

'Beaumont's right,' said Janet. 'He might like to come too, don't you think, John? Why don't you ask him?'

Of course we must, thought John. He saved Beaumont's life.

So one of the girls – Felicity, it was – was sent to fetch Mr Brown.

'We're moving house, Mr Brown,'

said John when the old mouse arrived. 'To get away from the cat.'

Just what I was thinking, said Mr Brown to himself.

'We're going to Number 16: there's no cat there,' said John.

'We wondered if you'd like to come with us,' said Janet.

'It's very kind of you, Mrs Robinson –'

'"Janet", please,' she interrupted.

'– very kind of you, er, Janet, as I was saying, but I'm sure you'd rather be on your own as a family. I shall miss you, of course.'

'No, you won't, Mr Brown,' said John in a masterful voice. 'I insist that you come with us. Please do.'

'We can't go without you, Uncle Brown,' said Beaumont quietly.

Uncle, thought the old mouse. How nice. Some of my seventy-eight children must, I hope, be alive and well but I never see any of them. They've all pushed off somewhere, so why don't I push off too?

'Please come, Uncle Brown!' squeaked the other mousekins.

'Pleeeease!' and then they heard the sound of the cat flap as the cat, attracted by all the noise, came into the kitchen.

Mr Brown looked at Janet and John and at Beaumont and the other five youngsters.

'Thank you,' he said. 'I'd love to.'

Chapter Four

Number 16 Simple Street did indeed smell quite strongly of mice, and the family who lived there wouldn't have dreamed of having a cat.

There were three giants (as mice thought of them): Mr Black, Mrs Black and their son, a boy called Bill.

Bill Black had always been keen on
pet animals, especially mice and, once
he was old enough, his parents let him
keep some. These were pet mice,
fancy mice, of course, not ordinary
housemice like the Robinsons and Mr
Brown.

Bill had mice of several different colours: he had white ones with pink eyes and white ones with black eyes and chocolate ones and fawn ones and plum-coloured ones and mice with special black markings called Dutch.

By the time Bill was ten years old, he had so many pet mice that his father and mother let him use a little spare room (which he called the Mousery) to keep all his different-coloured mice in their neat cages. By the time that Janet Robinson and her daughters had come into Number 16 to have a sniff around, there were thirty pet mice in the Mousery, not counting babies, so that the smell of them was pretty strong.

No matter, thought Janet. There's not the faintest smell of cat.

At the next full moon all the migrants made their move down the street from Number 24.

John Robinson – after politely asking the advice of old Mr Brown – had decided that though travelling in bright moonlight might be risky, it would alert them to any cats or other dangers on the way, and at midnight the emigration began.

John led the file of mice: behind him came Beaumont and Eustace and Ambrose. Next came Mr Brown, followed by Felicity and Desdemona and Camilla, while Janet brought up the rear.

After they'd gone a little way Beaumont said to his father, 'I'm just going to drop back to make sure Uncle B's all right.' It was just as well he did, for at that very moment a dog barked loudly from inside Number 22, and Mr Brown, frightened by the sudden noise, slipped off the pavement. He seemed to be about to cross the road.

'Come back! Come back! Quickly! Quickly!' cried Beaumont, and the old mouse obeyed just in time, for a car came roaring down the road, only just missing Mr Brown.

'Oh, thank you, Beaumont, my
boy!' he panted as he scrambled back
over the kerb. Another narrow squeak,
he thought. I save him from the cat,
he saves me from the car.

After that, they passed Numbers 20
and 18 – cat smells coming from both
these houses – and mercifully arrived

safely at Number 16 and made their way in. The scent of mice was everywhere but the nine travellers from Number 24 soon found the room where it was strongest: the Mousery.

The cages in which Bill Black kept his fancy mice stood on top of two long low tables. John Robinson shinned up the leg of one of them and found himself in front of the first cage, staring into the red eyes of a mouse that was otherwise pure white. It was a buck, John could tell from its scent, and a bad-tempered buck at that. Coming close to the bars of its cage it said in a sneery voice, 'Push off, you. We don't want common housemice in here. These cages are for well-bred fancy mice only, so sling your hook, ugly mug.'

'Don't talk to me like that!' said John angrily. 'Come on outside and

we'll see who's the better mouse.'

'Calm down, John,' said Mr Brown from the floor below. 'He can't come out anyway, he's in a cage.'

'Just as well for him,' said John.

'Yes, but just as well for us too,' said Mr Brown.

He turned to Janet.

'You've been very clever in your choice of house,' he said. 'One of the giants here keeps mice as pets, it would appear, so the place has got to be free of cats. Well done, my dear Janet.'

'Thank you, Mr Brown,' Janet replied. I can't call him by his first name, she thought, because I don't know what it is and I don't really like to ask him. Perhaps we'll never know what it is.

'There's lots of food about too,' she said.

'Which means,' said John, 'that there'll be lots of other housemice about,' and at that very moment a mouse came out through a hole in the skirting board.

'Too right, mate,' he said to John, 'but there's plenty for all of us. The giants here are lovely people, specially the smallest one of the three. No cats – as you can smell, no dogs, no traps, no poison, and they leave food all over the place. You've struck lucky, you lot. Welcome to Liberty Hall!'

Chapter Five

'He seemed a happy sort of chap,'
said John to Janet as the mouse
disappeared down its hole. 'Don't
you think so, Mr Brown?'

'I think,' said Mr Brown, 'that he
and his fellows have plenty to be
happy about. He's right – we have
struck lucky.'

For the rest of that night they all explored the Mousery. None of the fancy mice were as rude as the first pink-eyed white buck had been but all were a bit stand-offish.

'Hadn't we better be moving?' asked Janet as the first light of dawn came in through the window. 'We don't want one of the giants to come and find us in here.'

'Why not, Mum?' asked Beaumont.

'Because they might not wish to have nine more mice in their house,' said Janet. 'Let's all go down that hole in the skirting board and find where it leads to.'

So they all did. As they made their

way down, their sharp ears heard a lot
of mouse noises. There were runways
through which came sounds of mice,
above and below them. They came at
last to the cellar of Number 16 in
which there were a good many mice,
all of whom greeted the newcomers
in a friendly fashion.

Above their heads, Bill Black came
into the Mousery in his pyjamas (his
bedroom was next door) to give his
pets their breakfast. He filled the
feeding pot in each cage with canary
seed, made sure that all the mice had

clean water to drink and, of course, talked to the occupants of every cage. Bill was sure that pets like dogs and cats enjoyed being talked to, so why should mice be any different?

In the last cage was a chocolate doe, all by herself because she was soon to have babies. Bill took a very small bit of broken biscuit from a tin and put it down in front of her nose.

'D'you know,' he said to her, 'what I'd love to do? I'd love to tame a wild mouse. Shouldn't think anyone's ever done that. I'd have to catch one first though, a young one.' Even as he said these last words Bill heard a little scratching noise, and there, coming

out of the hole in the skirting board,
was a young housemouse.

Beaumont, the brightest, most
adventurous, and now indeed the
boldest of John and Janet's six
children, had heard the sound of Bill's
voice from the cellar below and had
scuttled back up the runway to see

what a giant looked like. Never in his short life had he seen one before.

How strange! thought Bill. Just the kind of mouse that I need, but how do I catch it?

Very slowly, he took another bit of biscuit from the tin. Very slowly, he moved towards the young mouse, who

crouched by the hole below, whiskers twitching. Very slowly, Bill Black offered the bit of biscuit to Beaumont Robinson.

They looked into each other's eyes and each had much the same feelings. They liked the look of one another.

This is a very bold little housemouse,

thought Bill. Could I make a pet of him?

This is a very nice giant, thought Beaumont. I'm not afraid of him at all.

He took a bite of biscuit.

'Delicious!' he said.

All Bill heard, of course, was a squeak, but it sounded like a happy squeak. Suddenly, the young mouse turned and disappeared down the hole.

'Dad!' cried Beaumont as he reached the cellar. 'There's ever such a nice giant up above us. He gave me a lovely bit of biscuit. Come up and see him!' and he turned and dashed up the runway again, followed by Ambrose and Camilla and

Desdemona and Eustace and Felicity.
After them went Janet, calling,
'Come back, children!' and after her
went John, calling, 'Come back, Janet!'
To his surprise Bill found himself
looking at five more mousekins, and

then to his astonishment two adult mice emerged from the hole.

Mum and Dad and six kids, he thought, and crumbled more biscuit on the floor. They were all feeding greedily when another mouse came up out of the hole, a mouse that, Bill could see, looked very old and was a bit wobbly on its legs. Immediately the mousekins surrounded it, squeaking happily.

Must be the grandfather, thought Bill. How could he know that they were all saying, 'Come on, Uncle Brown! Have some biscuit!' or that Janet and John were saying, 'Yes, help yourself, Mr Brown'?

The mice listened as the giant made noises. How could they know that he was saying, 'What a lovely family! Wherever did you come from? Would you like me to make you a special home, here in the Mousery? I don't mean a cage, I don't want to shut you up, but somewhere comfy and warm for you? How would you like that?'

Chapter Six

In fact the Robinson family and their friend Mr Brown never did get to live in the Mousery at Number 16. To be sure, they came up from the cellar whenever they heard the sound of Bill's voice as he talked to his pet mice. They knew he would always give

them something to eat. Beaumont was
the first of them who actually took
food from the giant's hand but the
others soon did too.

I wanted to tame a wild mouse,
thought Bill, and now it looks as
though I've tamed nine! And I dare
say there'll be more before long. I
must make a proper home for them.

So one day when the Robinsons and Mr Brown came up from the cellar, they found a large shallow box on the floor of the Mousery. Bill had put bedding in it, over which he had scattered a lot of canary seed, and by the time John Robinson and his family and his old friend had eaten it all, they felt quite at home.

So that when Janet said, 'Well, I suppose we'd better get back down to the cellar,' John said, 'Why?'

'It is very comfortable here, Janet,' said Mr Brown.

'Come on, Mum, let's stay,' said Beaumont.

'Yes, let's!' chorused Ambrose and Camilla and Desdemona and Eustace and Felicity.

So they did. But not for long
because soon two things happened.
First, the rapidly growing mousekins
decided that living with the pet mice
was a bit boring, so they went back to
the cellar where they could play with
their wild friends. Only Beaumont

stayed. He liked being with his friend the giant, and he was interested in getting to know the pet mice. He talked politely to them, and some of them responded in quite a friendly way.

The second thing to happen was that Janet had another lot of babies – nine this time: six boys and three girls.

Gilbert, Hermione, Inigo, Julius, Kingsley, Lindsay, Marmaduke, Niobe and Olivia.

'Only eleven to go, John,' said his old friend, out of Janet's hearing.

'What d'you mean, Mr Brown?' John asked.

'Eleven more and you'll have

finished your first alphabet of names.'

'Gosh!' said John, and 'Gosh!'
echoed Beaumont.

'I only hope,' said Mr Brown, 'that
I'm still around to see the alphabet
completed.'

'Why shouldn't you be, Uncle Brown?' asked Beaumont.

'Well, I'm not as young as I was.'

'You'll go on for ages yet, Mr Brown,' said John.

But he was wrong.

One morning a few days later, Bill woke up and went into the Mousery to look at what he thought of as his 'tame wild mice'. There were two boxes on the floor now, for Bill had supplied a small one as a single room for the mouse he thought of as 'Grandad'.

In the big box Bill could see Janet suckling her newborn nine, watched

by John and Beaumont. In the small
box Grandad lay comfortably, having
breakfast in bed. Not wanting to
disturb anyone, Bill tiptoed away.

Mr Brown spent a lot of his time
asleep, but he still had some appetite
and John and Beaumont brought him
choice bits of food.

As they had been collecting it that morning, Beaumont said, 'You always call Uncle Brown "Mr Brown", don't you, Dad? Why don't you use his first name?'

'I don't know it.'

'Can't you ask him?'

'I don't like to. He'd have told me if he'd wanted to.'

I'll ask him, thought Beaumont. I'm sure he wouldn't mind. He's nice, Uncle Brown is. He'll tell me his first name.

'Uncle Brown,' said Beaumont, climbing into the small box that afternoon. 'Will you tell me what your first name is? I'd like to know.'

The old mouse did not reply.

He has got a bit deaf lately, thought Beaumont, and more loudly he said, 'Uncle Brown! Can you hear me?'

But there was no answer.

With his nose Beaumont touched

the body of the old mouse. It was
stone cold.

Just then Bill came into the
Mousery with some bits of biscuit
that he'd saved as a treat for his
tame wild mice. He saw that one of
the youngsters was in Grandad's
box. It looked up at him and
squeaked.

'He's dead!' cried Beaumont. 'Look, giant, Uncle Brown is dead!'

Oh dear, thought Bill as he stood and stared down. Poor old Grandad.

Chapter Seven

All up and down, in both the even
and the odd-numbered houses in
Simple Street, mice were being born.
Mice were dying too, in the jaws of
cat or trap or of poisoning or simply
– like Mr Brown – of old age.

But never before had a mouse been

given such a funeral as he was.

'One thing I do know,' said Bill Black as he fed his fancy mice, 'and that is – I'm not just going to chuck poor old Grandad in the dustbin. He shall have a proper burial in the garden.'

Heaven only knows how Beaumont knew what was going on in the brain of his friend the young giant, but the fact remains that when Bill had dug a hole, he suddenly realized that there were seven little mourners at the graveside. Only Janet could not come out to pay her last respects.

'I can't leave the babies unprotected. Mr Brown wouldn't

have wanted me to,' she said to John.

But when Bill had carefully put the body in the grave, John and Ambrose and Beaumont and Camilla and Desdemona and Eustace and Felicity all crept to the edge for a last look at their old friend – 'Uncle' to them, 'Mr' always to John and Janet, and, had they known it, 'Grandad' to the giant who was shovelling the earth back over him.

That night Bill cleaned out the small box on the floor of the Mousery but left it where it was. It'll do for a spare room, he thought. When these nine new mousekins get too boisterous, their parents can get a bit of peace in it.

Time passed, and at Number 16 Gilbert, Hermione, Inigo, Julius, Kingsley, Lindsay, Marmaduke, Niobe

and Olivia went down to join their older brothers and sisters in all the fun and games that went on in the cellar.

John came out of the spare room and settled himself comfortably beside Janet in the big box.

'D'you think we shall have any more babies, dear?' he asked her.

'I shouldn't be at all surprised,' she replied.

The one member of the family who was different from the rest – as he always had been – was Beaumont. Once his father had left the spare room, he took it over, so as to be near his new friends.

Because he had grown so close to the young giant, Beaumont had seen a good deal of the fancy mice. He would go up and down the cages on

the low tables in the Mousery and
chat with them through the bars – the
pink-eyed whites, the black-eyed
whites, the chocolates, the fawns, the
plum-coloured mice and the Dutch
mice. Most were civil to him (even
the bad-tempered pink-eyed buck)
and, had he known it, quite a few of
the young does rather fancied this
friendly talkative young buck.

Bill noticed that his tame pet
housemouse spent a lot of time
looking and squeaking at one very
pretty plum-coloured doe. He offered
a bit of food to Beaumont, who came
on to the palm of the giant's hand as
usual, and then he popped him into an

empty cage and, catching the pretty
plum-coloured doe, put her in too.

One morning Bill woke to the sound of much squeaking from the big box on the Mousery floor.

'I want to be alone, John,' Janet was saying. 'Go away, please.'

'Why?'

'I'm going to have some more babies.'

'Gosh!' said John.

Don't have more than eleven, he thought, because then we'll reach the end of the alphabet, like Mr Brown said. How on earth am I to think of names beginning with X or Z? I'll ask Beaumont, he might know. But there was no sign of his son.

John climbed up and went along the tables, looking into each cage. In the

last one of all was a pretty little fancy
doe, a plum-coloured one, but she was
not alone.

'Beaumont!' cried John. 'What are
you doing in that cage?'

'Just having a chat with a friend,
Dad. I'll be out soon. How's Mum?'

'Having babies,' said John.

'Gosh!' said Beaumont.

When John returned later to the big box, Janet had had the babies.

'How many?' asked John.

'Eleven,' replied Janet.

As they spoke, Bill was letting his pet housemouse out of the fancy plum-coloured doe's cage, and soon Beaumont appeared.

'How on earth,' his father said to him out of Janet's hearing, 'am I going to think of names beginning with X or Z?'

'Easy, Dad,' said Beaumont. 'Just call it "Ecks" or "Zed", boy or girl. By the way, Dad,' he went on, 'I think you might like to know something, something that I guess Uncle Brown would have been pleased about.'

'What?' asked John.

'Before very long,' said Beaumont, 'I am going to be a dad, Dad.'

'Gosh!' said John Robinson. 'My whiskers! Fancy that! And you're right, Beaumont – Uncle Brown would have been very pleased. Gosh!'

Dick King-Smith

No. 1 for animal magic!

'Why can't I learn to be a sheep-pig?'

Babe wants to learn everything he needs to know to be a sheep-dog. He knows he can't be a real sheep-dog. But maybe, just maybe, he might be a sheep-PIG!

'A thrilling, funny, charmer of a book'
– *Guardian*

'Dick King-Smith is a huge favourite'
– *Observer*

Winner of the Guardian Fiction Award

Dick King-Smith
The Sheep-Pig

Illustration © Chris Riddell

Puffin by Post

The Mouse Family Robinson – Dick King-Smith

If you have enjoyed this book and want to read more,
then check out these other great Puffin titles.
You can order any of the following books direct with Puffin by Post:

The Sheep-Pig • Dick King-Smith • 9780141316000	£4.99
The classic tale of Babe that became a blockbuster film	

The Fox Busters • Dick King-Smith • 9780141316420	£4.99
'Our leading author of farmyard stories' – *Telegraph*	

The Jenius • Dick King-Smith • 9780141312866	£4.99
'He is a great storyteller' – *Yorkshire Post*	

George Speaks • Dick King-Smith • 9780141316406	£3.99
'His animal stories never descend to fluffiness' – *Independent on Sunday*	

Martin's Mice • Dick King-Smith • 9780141317540	£4.99
'His very name guarantees quality' – *Guardian*	

Just contact:

Puffin Books, C/o Bookpost, PO Box 29,
Douglas, Isle of Man, IM99 1BQ
Credit cards accepted. For further details:
Telephone: 01624 677237
Fax: 01624 670923

You can email your orders to: bookshop@enterprise.net
Or order online at: www.bookpost.co.uk

Free delivery in the UK.
Overseas customers must add £2 per book.

Prices and availability are subject to change.

Visit puffin.co.uk to find out about the latest titles, read extracts and
exclusive author interviews, and enter exciting competitions.
You can also browse thousands of Puffin books online.